"Dedicated to the people of Ladakh. Jullay!"

- Praba Ram & Sheela Preuitt

THUKPA FOR ALL

Praba Ram & Sheela Preuitt

Shilpa Ranade

Gonggg...
rings the gong at the gompa.
Tsering perks up and sets off home.

Tikk, tuckk...
Tsering treks with his stick, sweeping it left and right.
His taste buds tingle. Abi's noodle soup beckons.

He hums,

Hot, hot thukpa
Hearty, chunky thukpa
Yummy, spicy thukpa

Flap, thwap...
Prayer flags flutter.
Tsering moves faster, tapping the stick as he walks.

"Jullay, my friend! What's the hurry?" asks Rigzin,
making way for Tsering.

"Going home for Abi's thukpa, the best thukpa in town!"
answers Tsering brightly.

"Sounds delicious," says Rigzin longingly.

"Would you like to join us?" invites Tsering.

"Sure! I'll be there," shouts Rigzin.

Cruck, crunch...

Tsering walks down the familiar gravel trail.

Baa baa...

A lamb bleats in his path.

"Molu, did you sneak off from Tashi uncle's patch again?"
he asks, picking her up and stroking her fur.

"There's my wandering sheep!" says Tashi uncle, gathering
little Molu in his arms. "You always bring her back, Tsering.
Thank you," he says, guiding him back to the trail.

As he walks away, Tsering calls out, "It's been a long time since
you visited us, uncle. Abi is making thukpa tonight. Please come."

"I'd love to. Tell Abi that I will be there," replies Tashi uncle.

Gurgle, burble...

'Almost home,' thinks Tsering.

"Jullay, Tsering. What's the hurry?"
calls out Neema aunty from the washing stream.

"Abi's thukpa, aunty. Come have dinner with us.
Abi will be glad to see you," replies Tsering.
"I'll be there, Tsering," assures Neema aunty.

Cough, sniffle...

It's his neighbor Norboo me-me.
"Your cough sounds worse, me-me,"
says Tsering. "Abi's thukpa will make
it better. Come have some this evening."
"Yes, it will. I will see you in a few
hours," says Norboo me-me.

Krutt, kruk...
Abi is working in the garden.

"Abi-le, I told Rigzin that your thukpa is the best.
He is coming to eat with us tonight," declares Tsering.

"Rigzin is always welcome," smiles Abi.

"Oh, by the way, Tashi uncle and Neema aunty are coming too. And Norboo me-me as well," adds Tsering excitedly.

"All of them? For tonight? My dear boy! We need more water... hmm... vegetables and noodles too. Let me see what I can do." Abi starts bustling around.

"Bring me some peas for the soup," she adds, handing Tsering a basket.

Tsering shuffles along the stone
wall to the vegetable patch.

He feels the smooth pea pods with
his fingers and plucks a basketful.

Back at the porch, he carefully
squeezes each pod on the seams.
Little round peas slide into his cupped palm.

Tring, tringg... goes the bell.

"Ah, Rigzin, there you are!" says Tsering.
"Welcome to our home."

"You know my cycle bell so well, Tsering," says Rigzin.
"Here, Ama-le sent some water and cheese."

"Thank you, Rigzin, you didn't have to," says Tsering.

Cough, cough...

"Norboo me-me, you came! Are you feeling better?"
asks Tsering gently.

"Yes, Tsering. Thank you," Norboo me-me replies.
"I have brought some spinach for Abi.
Here, take it to her."

Cling, clang... tinkle some bracelets.

"Neema aunty?" calls out Tsering.

"Yes, Tsering," says Neema aunty. "I have brought apricot jam and some freshly kneaded dough for the noodles."

"And here's a flask of buttered tea," says Tashi uncle.

Tsering takes everything to Abi.

"Plenty for all," she beams.

Abi chops onions and tomatoes.
Just as the mustard oil gets smoky in the brass pot...

"Oh no, the power went out! It's so dark,"
complains Rigzin.

"It's a little early for a power cut,"
adds Neema aunty.

"Not much moonlight either,"
observes Norboo me-me.

"How will I finish making my thukpa?"
Abi worries aloud, as she adds the
onions and tomatoes to the pot.

"Lights on or off doesn't matter to me, Abi-le," says
Tsering as he saunters closer to Abi. "I'll help you."

"Cumin, pepper, and garam masala,"
calls out Abi.

Tsering sniffs the spice jars on the shelf
and hands them to her one by one.

Abi adds the spices and continues to
stir the pot for a few minutes.

"Spinach and peas now," says Abi.
Tsering pats the table top. The leaves
and the basket of peas brush his fingers.

"Right here, Abi-le," he hands them to her.

"The jug of water?" Abi asks.

"Here you go, Abi-le," says Tsering,
passing her the jug.

Abi stirs as the soup comes to a boil.

Soon the aroma of thukpa fills the house.

Tsering hums,

Hot, hot thukpa
Hearty, chunky thukpa
Yummy, spicy thukpa

Abi's noodle soup is almost ready.

"Is it time for the noodles, Abi-le?"
asks Tsering excitedly.

"Yes, perfect timing, Tsering,"
she smiles.

Tsering picks up the fresh dough
that Neema aunty has brought.

"I will help make some too," insists
Neema aunty, stumbling to the table.

Tsering rolls the dough as flat as
he can with the rolling pin,
and starts tearing strips.

"The power is back!" Rigzin calls out.

"Just in time," says Abi, dropping the noodles
into the simmering pot of soup.

"Look, Tsering has made perfect-looking noodles,
all exactly the same," remarks Abi.

"These oddly shaped ones are my work,"
says Neema aunty, chuckling.

"Tsering's thukpa is the best in town," says Rigzin.
Tsering smiles his biggest, widest smile.

Abi's noodle soup is served.

Laughter echoes through the mountain air.

Hot, hot thukpa
Hearty, chunky thukpa
Yummy, spicy thukpa

A GLIMPSE INTO LADAKHI LIFE

Ladakh is a cold desert located in the state of Jammu and Kashmir in India. Gompas or monasteries, which form an important architectural aspect of the region, dot the landscape of Ladakh. One can see prayer flags and prayer wheels everywhere. Both men and women engage in physical labor and work-related differences are uncommon. They live in stone houses, and many have vegetable gardens in the front yard. People farm throughout the year except during winter months.

Water is scarce and flows from glaciers as small streams. There are streams specific to drinking, and streams that are used only for washing. Ladakhis believe strongly in reuse and recycling, and find multiple uses for limited natural resources.

The Ladakhis are very hospitable people, and community feasts are common. Buttered tea, apricot jam, and homemade cheese are unique to their cuisine. Thukpa is a simple noodle soup that is a staple in the Northern Himalayan regions of Tibet, Ladakh, and Nepal, with many variations.

GLOSSARY

Abi: Grandma. "le" is added for respect as in Abi-le. Ama-le is mother.

Jullay: Hello or thank you. A common phrase in Ladakhi language.

Me-me: Elderly man addressed respectfully.

Thukpa: Noodle soup with vegetables and flavoring.

Thukpa for Two

Ingredients

1 cup of vegetables, cut into chunks (cauliflower, potatoes, mushrooms, carrots)

½ cup of chopped spinach

½ cup of peas

2 onions, chopped

4 stems of spring onions, coarsely chopped

Coriander leaves, finely chopped

½ lemon, juiced

1 tablespoon oil

1 tablespoon ginger and garlic, minced

1 tablespoon cumin powder

1 teaspoon red chili powder

1 teaspoon garam masala

Salt and pepper to taste

Handful of rice or wheat noodles

6 cups of water

Method

1. In a large saucepan, heat the oil; sauté the onions, garlic and ginger, spring onions and spice powders; cook till it is aromatic and the onions turn translucent.

2. Now add vegetables and 3 cups of water; simmer till vegetables turn tender but not too mushy; add lemon juice and season with salt and pepper.

3. In another vessel, bring 3 cups of water to boil.

4. Drop in the noodles and boil till cooked.

5. Drain the noodles and put half the noodles in each bowl.

6. Ladle the vegetables and the liquid stock over the cooked noodles.

7. Top with coriander leaves, and enjoy hot thukpa - Tibetan Noodle Soup!

PRAISE FOR THUKPA FOR ALL

"…a beautiful story of give and take in a community…That Tsering is blind is woven subtly into the story. Everyone around him accepts it and you do too, because that becomes beside the point."
— **Saffron Tree**

"Thukpa For All brings Ladakh to life. The beautifully rendered illustrations show the natural splendor of this cold desert located in Jammu and Kashmir."
— **Booked for Life**

"…the story beautifully weaves in the point that specially abled children are no different from others though they can stun others with their unexpected capabilities."
— **Mums and Stories**

"The story is simple and heartwarming, with a message of friendship and generosity."
— **The Book Chief**

Thukpa For All

© and ℗ 2018 Karadi Tales Company Pvt. Ltd.

First reprint January 2019

Text: Praba Ram & Sheela Preuitt
Illustrations: Shilpa Ranade

Karadi Tales Company Pvt. Ltd.
3A Dev Regency, 11 First Main Road,
Gandhinagar, Adyar, Chennai 600020
Tel.: +91-44-42054243
email: contact@karaditales.com
www.karaditales.com

ISBN: 978-81-9338-898-3

Distributed in the United States by Consortium Book Sales & Distribution
www.cbsd.com

Cataloging - in - Publication information:

Printed and bound in India by Manipal Technologies Limited, Manipal

Ram, Praba & Preuitt, Sheela
Thukpa For All / Praba Ram & Preuitt Sheela; illustrated by Shilpa Ranade
p.32; color illustrations; 24.5 x 24 cm.

JUV000000 JUVENILE FICTION / General
JUV050000 JUVENILE FICTION / Cooking & Food
JUV009050 JUVENILE FICTION / Concepts / Senses & Sensation
JUV039150 JUVENILE FICTION / Disabilities & Special Needs
JUV039060 JUVENILE FICTION / Social Themes / Friendship
JUV074000 JUVENILE FICTION / Diversity & Multicultural

Praba Ram

Sheela Preuitt

Praba Ram & **Sheela Preuitt** love stories of all sorts. When they are not seeking wisdom from their fuzzy-tailed feline friends, their other *purr-suits* include concocting soups from varied cuisines, growing seasonal vegetables, and supporting childhood literacy in their community.

Praba works with children via book clubs, art appreciation workshops, and writing groups. She has a Master's in Public Policy from UCLA. Day-time coder and night-time writer, Sheela also volunteers as a reading specialist at her kids' school. She holds a Master's in Science Education.

Shilpa Ranade is an animator and illustrator. She is a Professor in the Animation programme at IDC School Of Design, IIT Mumbai. She works in the area of creating content for children and has illustrated numerous books for leading publishers and has been making animated films. Her films have won accolades at some of the most prestigious film festivals in the world.

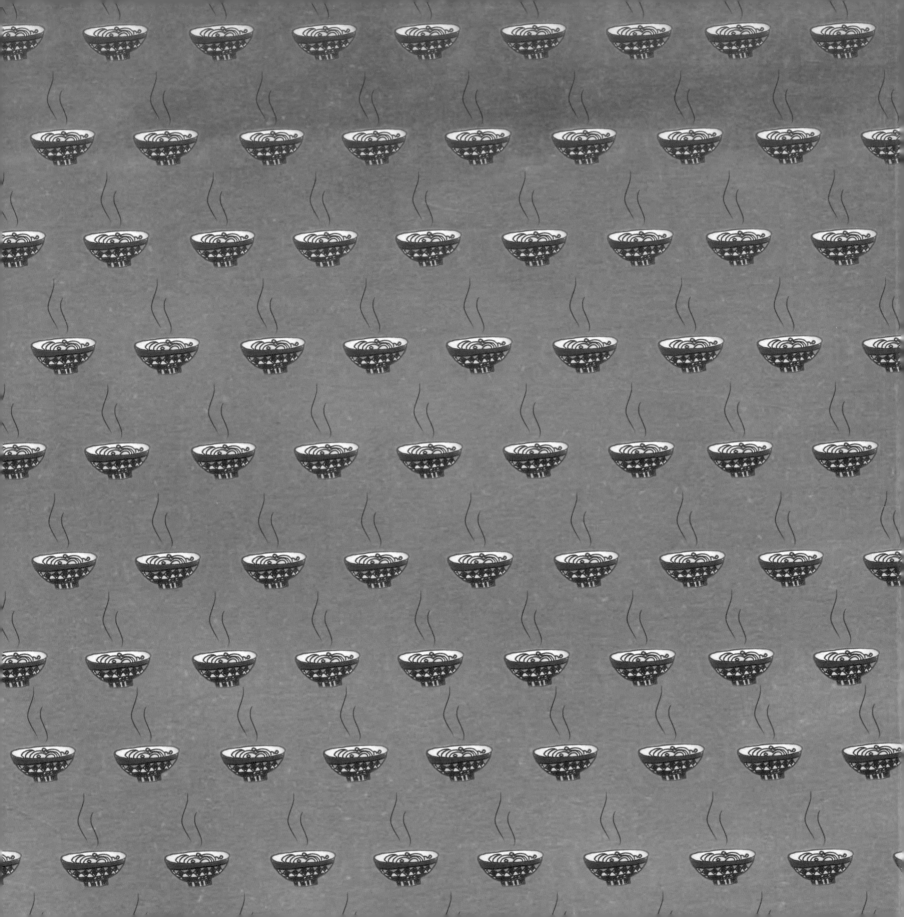